YOKO

ROSEMARY WELLS

Disney • HYPERION BOOKS
NEW YORK

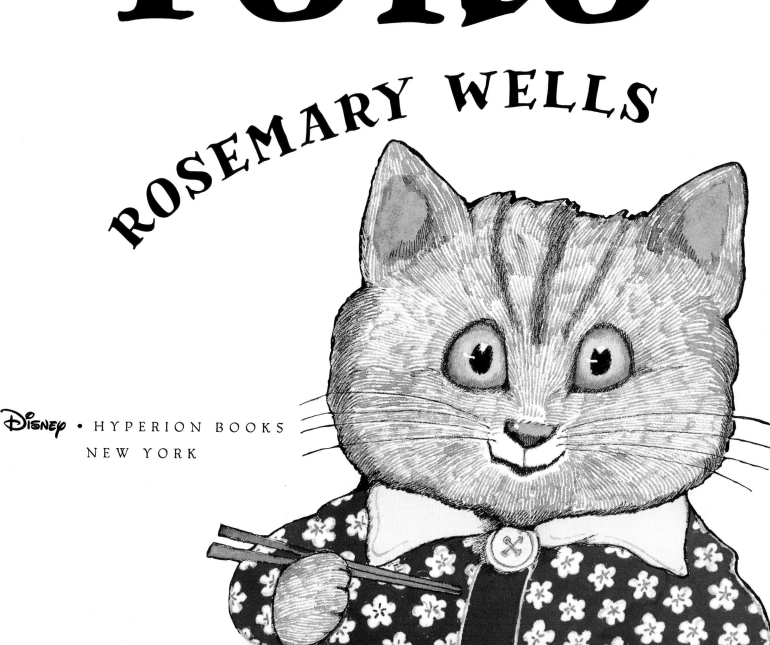

Published by Disney • Hyperion Books, an imprint of Disney Book Group. No part

of this book may be reproduced or transmitted in any form or by any means, electronic

or mechanical, including photocopying, recording, or by any information storage and

retrieval system, without written permission from the publisher. For information address

Disney • Hyperion Books, 114 Fifth Avenue, New York, New York 10011-5690.

First Disney • Hyperion paperback edition, 2009

3 5 7 9 10 8 6 4

F850-6835-5-11258
Printed in Singapore

Library of Congress Cataloging-in-Publication Data on file.

ISBN 978-1-4231-1983-8

Visit www.hyperionbooksforchildren.com

The author wishes to thank Junko Yokota.

What would you like for lunch today,
my little cherry blossom?" asked Yoko's mother.
"All my favorite things, please," answered Yoko.

Yoko's mother spread steamed rice on a bamboo mat. She rolled up a secret treasure inside each piece. Then she packed it all in a willow-covered cooler.

"Have a wonderful day at school, my little
cherry blossom," said Yoko's mother.
"I will!" answered Yoko.

Yoko said hello to all her friends. Everyone in
Mrs. Jenkins's class sang the Good Morning Song.

At noon Mrs. Jenkins rang the lunch bell. "Lunch
boxes out and open, please, boys and girls!" said
Mrs. Jenkins.

Timothy unwrapped a peanut butter and honey sandwich. Valerie had cream cheese and jelly.

Fritz had a meatball grinder. Tulip had
Swiss cheese on rye.

Hazel had egg salad on pumpernickel.
Doris had squeeze cheese on white,

and the Franks had franks and beans.

Yoko opened the willow-covered cooler. Inside was her favorite sushi. Tucked in the rice rolls were the crispiest cucumber, the pinkest shrimp, the greenest seaweed, and the tastiest tuna.

"What's in your lunch?" asked one of the Franks.
"Ick! It's green! It's seaweed!"

"Oh, no!" said the other Frank.
"Don't tell me that's raw fish!"

"Watch out! It's moving!" said Doris.
"Yuck-o-rama!" said Tulip and Fritz.

Valerie blew the playtime whistle.
"Everybody out!" said Valerie.

Yoko did not want to play ball or swing on the swings.
"What's wrong, Yoko?" asked Mrs. Jenkins.

"Everybody laughed at my lunch," answered Yoko.
"They'll forget about it by snack time," said Mrs. Jenkins.

But they didn't. During the *Snack Time Song*,
Yoko opened a thermos cup of red bean ice cream.

"Red bean ice cream is for weirdos!" snorted the Franks.
Mrs. Jenkins switched to the *Friendly Song*.

Mrs. Jenkins knew the Friendly Song was not enough. Late into the evening she fretted about Yoko. Finally the answer came to her.

HILLTOP SCHOOL

Dear Parents,

Monday will be International Food Day at Hilltop School. Everyone is asked to bring in a dish from a foreign country. Everyone must try a bite of everything!

Happy cooking!
Mrs. Jenkins

"We will make a deluxe sushi for the whole class!"
said Yoko's mother. "Don't worry, my little
cherry blossom, everyone will try our sushi and
everyone will love it!"

On Monday morning Valerie and her mother carried in a plate of enchiladas.

Timothy and his mother made Caribbean
coconut crisps.

Hazel brought
Nigerian nut soup.

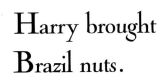

Harry brought
Brazil nuts.

Doris brought
Irish stew.

Tulip brought
potato knishes.

Monica brought
a pitcher of
mango smoothies.

Fritz brought
spaghetti.

Big Frank cooked up a pot of Boston franks and beans.

At noon Mrs. Jenkins rang the lunch bell and everyone sang the Clean Hands Song.

"What does International Food Day mean to us, boys and girls?" asked Mrs. Jenkins. "Try everything!" said everybody.

When Valerie blew the playtime whistle, there was not
a nibble of nuts or a sip of smoothie left.

But no one had touched even one piece of
Yoko's sushi.

Yoko sat under the Learning Tree.
Suddenly she heard the clickety-click of chopsticks.

It was Timothy. He was still hungry.

"Let me show you how," said Yoko.

Timothy polished off the rest of the crab cones his own way.

"Can we have sushi again tomorrow?" he said.
"I'll ask my mother," answered Yoko.

During the School Bus Song, Timothy found a
coconut crisp in his pocket. He gave it to Yoko.
"It's even better than red bean ice cream!" said Yoko.

On the bus Timothy and Yoko made plans to push their desks together and open a restaurant the very next day.

And they did. They ordered
tomato sandwiches and dragon rolls.

For dessert they had brownies with
green tea ice cream. And they couldn't
have asked for anything more.